Pegasus Princesses
SPECIAL EDITION
Eight in One Book Collection
Written and Illustrated By Arielle Namenyi

VOLUMES:

Pegasus Princesses

Order Of The Princesses

Once in a land far, far away stood the magical kingdom of Friesia. Friesia was a place where the pegasus lived in harmony, spending their time completeing tasks for the King. One of these little pegasus was named Diamond. She was a cute little pegasus that loved to fly in the clouds and dream of adventures.

One day, Diamond recieved a royal letter in the mail. It said: "Your presence is requested this evening on behalf of Prince Morning Star at his castle."

That night, Diamond was escorted into the prince's castle. After being taken to the throne room, Diamond was surprised to find six other young pegasus standing before the prince's seat. Diamond walked next to one of the young pegasus.
"My name is Jade." The pegasus introduced. Suddenly a trumpet blew and in walked Prince Morning Star. The pegasus reverently bowed as he approached them.

6.

"I'm sure you all wonder why you have been summoned here tonight." He announced. "The King has asked me to choose seven young pegasus to take on a difficult task." Diamond and Jade shot a glance at each other, uneasy and confused about what would happen next.

Suddenly a burst of clouds molded in front of the prince and they jumped back. "My father once had a second in command pegasus who was granted much power and beauty." As Prince Morning Star spoke the clouds molded the story he was telling.

"This pegasus was called Natas. But Natas wasn't happy with his position. He wanted to be king. So he tricked many of my father's subjects and rose up against him. Natas failed to overthrow the kingdom, and my father banished him. Natas' pride soon deformed him into a horrid beast, who is now better known as the Dragon of Chaos. He is still determined to overthrow my father, and he and his followers try with all their might to trick everyone to go against everything my father, the King, has built."

"If I may ask, where do we fit in with all of this, my Lord?" Diamond asked.

"Chaos' demons are infecting every city. I need you to go and show everyone that my father is still here, and he loves his subjects and is calling them to resist Chaos and be loyal to us."

"But he is such a good king. How could anyone..."

"Chaos is very powerful and very smart. He can convince even the most loyal subjects. That's why we need you."

"What can we do?" One of the other pegasus asked. "We're not strong and, no offense, but we're also nobodies."

"Speak for yourself!" Snapped a young red pegasus.

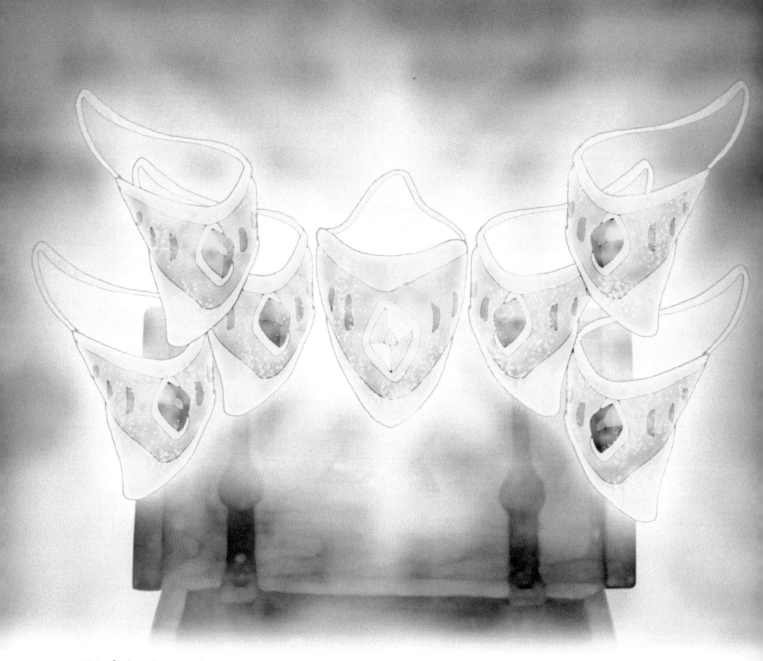

"My father has created seven magical stones. Within them is the power to defeat the work of Chaos." Suddenly an eagle flew in with a box and dropped it on the ground. The box unlatched and a blinding light escaped. Diamond shielded her eyes and slowly looked back. Seven beautiful breastplates with gemstones were floating above them.

"Princess Jade." Morning Star started.
"Princess?!" Jade exclaimed.
"You are given the gift of joy." One of the breastplates clasped around Jade's chest and lit up with power.

11.

"Princess Ruby... the gift of humbleness."

"Princess Amber, the gift of patience."

13.

"Princes Sapphire, the gift of courage."

"Princess Amethyst, the gift of faith."

15.

"Princess Topaz, the gift of mercy."

16.

"And Princess Diamond." Diamond looked up. "Your gift is the most powerful of all. The gift of love." The last breastplate stone, a beautiful diamond, clasped around her chest as light beamed out. "You are now all royal sisters. You shall work together to defeat Chaos and his minions." The seven looked at each other. "But there is one thing you should know before you go. The stones will only work if you stay true to your gifts. If you resist Chaos and stay on the side of the King, you will not fail." And with that the girls were escorted out of the castle.

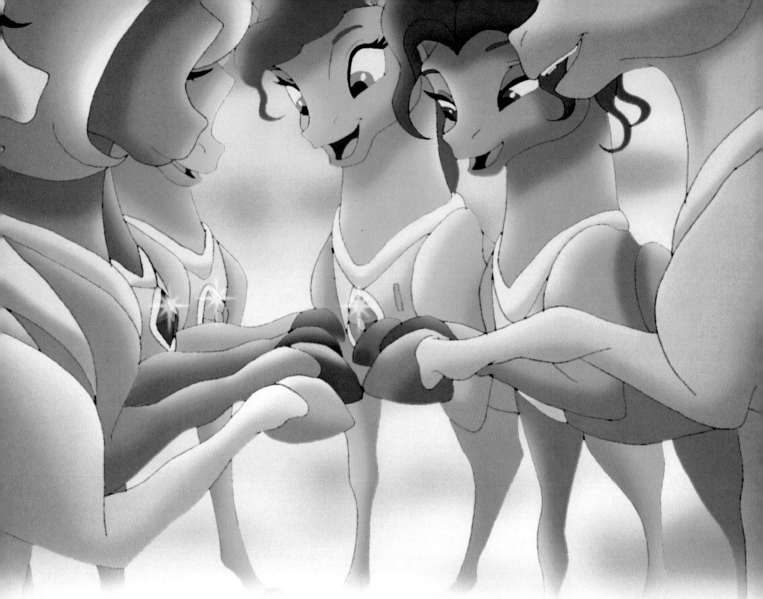

"I can't believe I'm a princess!" Ruby exclaimed excitedly.

"Don't be so excited. This is a lot of responsibility." Amber frowned.

"Who are we? We're just seven little pegasus. How can we stand up to Chaos?" Amethyst sighed.

"But we have power from the King, not our own. Morning Star is counting on us." Diamond spoke up.

"Diamond is right!" Jade stepped forward. "Let's make a pact! Let's promise to stick together as sisters and use our stones to stay true to our king!" "Here here!" Ruby called out while holding out her hoof. The others put their hooves in too and exclaimed "Here here!"

"Now what?" Amber asked. "Should we just go and find this Chaos guy?"

"Or maybe *he* will find us." Topaz commented, looking off. They all followed her gaze and noticed a dark cloud spreading over Friesia.

"That doesn't look good." Sapphire whimpered.

"It's a wonder why Prince Morning Star ever gave you the gift of courage." Amber blurted.

"It's a wonder why you got patience." Ruby huffed while flinging her hair.

"It seems like all our powers are also the weakest parts of our personality." Said Topaz.

"Not me!" Jade jumped happily.

"Or me." Ruby added. They all looked at her, quiet.

"Let's keep a lookout girls. Something tells me that cloud is something not good." Diamond said while starting into the city.

As the princesses entered the village square, they noticed everyone gathering together. Diamond looked up and saw a pegasus standing above the crowd. "I've never seen him before." Diamond whispered to herself.

"A mysterious newcomer... he is dreamy!" Ruby sighed.

"Never fear!" The pegasus called out to the crowd. "I have been sent by the King to keep you all safe! I have powerful stones for everyone that will give you power to keep you safe and do whatever your heart desires!" The princesses looked up and saw breastplates similar to theirs.

"He must be from the king if he has those!" Ruby shouted. Soon everyone started crowding around the new pegasus, waiting to get their own stones.

"Wait a second!" Diamond called out. "Where did you get these stones?"

"Why, I made them myself. I see you already have your own. I can offer you better and stronger ones if you want."

"But that doesn't make sense." Topaz commented.

"It makes perfect sense to me." Ruby said excitedly. "Who wants to have the dreadful stone of humbleness? What can you offer me, handsome?"

"I have just the stone for you." He said while picking out a breastplate.

"The gift of fame. With this breast plate you can be a celebrity and be famous and everyone everywhere will love you. All you need to do is trade your old stone with this one."

"Sounds fair enough." Ruby agreed. "Fame sounds much more attractive than being humble."

"Don't you dare!" Amber shouted while blocking Ruby. "You're not from the King! Morning Star told us nothing about you!"

"On the contrary... we've actually heard much about you." Topaz frowned.

"Topaz is right! I'm sure Chaos sent you here to confuse the town!"

Everyone was quiet, waiting for what the pegasus had to say.

"False accusations." The pegasus chuckled. "I wasn't sent by Chaos. I *am* Chaos." Suddenly the pegasus morphed into a frightening fire-breathing dragon. "So it is me! Does it matter? You either fall by my wrath or taste the goodness I have to offer!"

"You can't defeat us! We have power from the King!" Diamond told him.

"Show me! Let's see you measure up to me!" Chaos spit fire and Diamond jumped out of the way.

"Come on girls! Let's use our stones!" Diamond called out.

The seven stood in the line and waited for their stones to do the work... but nothing happened.

"Nothing's happening." Amethyst said.

"I told you!" Chaos laughed. "You are worth nothing against me!"

"I'm getting really impatient right now!" Amber stomped with her hoof.

"Wait. Hold on a second..." Diamond thought. "You guys, the stones aren't working because we are not staying true to our gifts! Amber, calm down!" Diamond looked over and saw Sapphire cowering behind a crate. "Sapphire, you need to be brave! Everyone, let's work together!"

"How can we work together with someone like Amber a part of our group?" Ruby sneered.

"This is impossible!" Amethyst sighed.

"No, you need to have faith Amethyst!" Diamond told her.

"We can do this!" Everyone turned around and saw Jade standing there.

"We have power from the King and we have instructions from him. We can't fail as long as we follow his word!" Suddenly Jade's stone started glowing.

"Look at her stone!" Topaz said. "It's working!"

Diamond turned toward Chaos and frowned. "Let's do this!"

Slowly each stone began to light up as the pegasus began to use their gifts. Light admitted from the stones and shone straight toward Chaos. He blew fire out of his mouth and stopped the light. "I don't get it." Diamond said.

"Why isn't it working?"

"Where's Sapphire?" Jade asked. They looked around and Amethyst found her hiding behind the crate still.

"Sapphire, you need to come help us! Don't be afraid! We need you!" She told her. "I can't do it!" Sapphire cried. "I'm just a little pegasus. I'm scared!"

"You need to have faith in the power of the King." Amethyst told her.

"He won't let anything happen to us as long as we trust in him."

25.

Amethyst helped Sapphire up and brought her back to the group.

"Are you ready?" She asked.

"I think so." Sapphire whispered.

"Then let's go!" Amber called out. Each of their stones started lighting up again and the light shone toward Chaos. Chaos just laughed and put his hand out to stop the light. Suddenly he pulled back and yelled in pain. He grabbed his hand and looked back at the girls. "It's working!" Diamond called out. "Keep going!"

Chaos furiously started throwing fiery darts at them, but they stood ground. The crowd around them ran away and took cover. All the girls were tempted to give in, but they all looked at each other and knew that they had to do what Prince Morning Star asked them to.

After a while, Chaos backed up and angrily called out, "You have not won! I'll be back!" And with that, he disappeared as fast as he came and the skies became clear again. The villagers came out and cheered. "You all need to be careful and watch for Chaos and his minions. Stay true to the King and don't give in!" Diamond told them. "Do you think he will really be back?" Sapphire asked.

"I'm sure he will." Diamond told her. "But we'll be ready for him."

Later, in a faraway kingdom, Chaos gathered his minions.
"It's no use, my Lord." One of them said. "Those stones are just too powerful."
"The stones may be powerful..." Chaos commented. "But they cannot be used if those princesses don't stay true to their gifts. Make sure they get discouraged." And from that day on, Chaos and his minions plotted on how to deceive the Pegasus Princesses.

Story Reflections

*"Then said Jesus to them again, Peace be unto you:
as my Father hath sent me, even so send I you."*
-John 20:21

Just like Morning Star sent the Pegasus Princesses to use their gifts to help others and fight Chaos, so does Jesus send us to go out and be a light to this world, destorying Satan's darkeness.

Like the pegasus girls, Jesus adopts us into His family making us royal princes and princesses and by doing so giving the gift of His Holy Spirit. We can't fight sin and Satan alone, but with the power that God gives us we will never fail.

Many times Satan comes as "an angel of light" and is able to decieve us, but if we stay close to God and get to know Him we will be able to discern if the voices we hear are from Satan or God.

Many times when we feel like we are at our weakest point is when God is able to have His power shine through us. We are able to conquer anything with the power He gives us as long as we believe.

*""Therefore I take pleasure in infirmities, in reproaches, in necessities,
in persecutions, in distresses for Christ's sake:
for when I am weak, then am I strong."*
-2 Corinthians 12:10

DIAMOND

Princess Of Love

2

"Oh, I feel my hair starting to frizz already!" Ruby puffed while trying to pin up a banner.

"I don't see why we have to make such a big fuss just because your brother is coming to town." Amber scoffed while holding up the other end of the banner.

"I'm actually excited to meet Ruby's brother." Jade smiled while setting up the fondue fountain.

"You should be." Ruby said while flipping her hair. "He is the best! Oh... where is Diamond when you need her?"

"Probably daydreaming up in the clouds somewhere." Topaz commented while arranging chairs.
"I don't think she even knows we're planning for your brother's visit, Ruby. Sapphire
isn't here either."
"For heaven's sake, I thought I told you to round up the crew Amber!" Ruby frowned.
"I don't have the nerve to be your service pegasus. You have a problem, you go find them!" Amber
told her.
"Huh! Then maybe I will! I need a break anyways!" And with that, Ruby soared away into the clouds.

Ruby only had to fly for a little while before she spotted Diamond in the distance, molding some clouds.
"What are you up to?" Ruby asked as she landed.
"Oh, hi Ruby!" Diamond greeted. "I'm cloud sculpting! I can imagine one day sculpting for all sorts of events! I figure as long as I practice and try hard I can start building up a portfolio!"
"I have an idea how to help you." Ruby said. "My brother is coming to town tonight and he is a journalist. We all have been setting up an event for his homecoming and it would be lovely if you made a cloud sculpture for him. You never know what could happen from that."

"Oh, would you really let me sculpt clouds for the event? That would be a great experience!"
"Of course. Just remember to get it done by 5 PM tonight at the Garden Square. You can do anything that seems fitting... surprise me!" And with that Ruby swooped off.
"Wow, this is great!" Diamond thought. "My dream of becoming a well-known cloud sculptor might come true!" Diamond did a few flips of excitement and then calmed down. "I know where to get the best clouds for this project!" She announced. "Sunset Valley!"

Diamond was so excited to impress Ruby and her brother with her cloud sculpture. She flew into Sunset Valley to find some good cloud material for her sculpture, but she noticed something in the distance. Diamond quickly flew over and peeked out from behind a cloud and was surprised at what she saw. There, before her very eyes was the most beautiful cloud sculptures she had ever seen. "I wonder who made these." Diamond thought aloud.

Suddenly she heard a faint voice singing and decided to lay low to see what it was. Soon Sapphire emerged from behind one of the clouds and began sculpting while she was singing.

"Sapphire?!" Diamond exclaimed. Sapphire jumped back and darted behind a cloud.

"Sorry to scare you! It's just me... Diamond!"

"Oh... hi Diamond." Sapphire shyly greeted as she emerged from behind the cloud.

"Did you make all of these yourself?" Diamond asked.

"I did." Sapphire admitted. "I know they're not that good but I love sculpting clouds."

"Are you kidding me? They are amazing!"

"You really think so?"

"For sure! You could get a good job with work like this!"

"That's my dream to become a good cloud sculptor… but I'm afraid I don't know where to start."

Diamond's heart tugged within her. She knew that Ruby's event would be a perfect start for Sapphire to display her beautiful artwork, but at the same time Diamond wanted to make the sculpture for the event.

Diamond figured it was better not to say anything at the moment. "Ruby's brother is coming tonight and she is throwing a little party for him. Are you coming?"
"I don't know..."
"You should. I'll see you tonight at five in Garden Square!"

The girls didn't know it, but one of Chaos' minions was spying on them, listening in on their conversation.
"What a golden opportunity." He slyly sneered. "A work of deception could not be easier."
Then he quietly followed Diamond as she headed to the Garden Square.

"I wanted to see what you thought." Diamond said after she told Ruby about Sapphire. "I would love to be a cloud sculptor but I feel bad for Sapphire. She clearly has a gift."

As soon as Ruby was about to answer, Chaos' minion entered her stone. She shook her head and stepped back.

"Are you all right?" Diamond asked.

"Of course. I was just thinking... why would you worry about Sapphire? You're the one with the dream and you're the one I asked to sculpt clouds for my brother's party. If Sapphire was meant to sculpt for this event then she would have asked me. It's not your fault that she is too afraid to put herself out there." Ruby answered.

Diamond was taken aback by her straightforwardness, but at the same time deep inside she really wanted to agree with Ruby. "If I really think about it... you do have a point. Even if Sapphire would sculpt for this event, she's too frail to make it out there as a sculptor. It's not bad that I have the same dream as her. I'm sure she won't think twice about me becoming a sculptor as well."

"That's exactly what I say!" Ruby agreed. "We got to look out for ourselves and build ourselves up the ladder!"

"Thanks Ruby. I can't thank you enough for this opportunity."
"Just go finish the sculpture before it's too late."
Diamond nodded and took off. The evil minion chuckled and slid out of Ruby's stone. She shook her head and looked up at Diamond flying away. "That's strange." She said to herself. "I just had the most massive brain fog. I have no idea what we were talking about. I'm sure it's not important."
And with that she went back to managing the event for her brother's arrival.

Later on, Diamond began sculpting a sculpture for Ruby's party.
"What should I make?" Diamond thought. Suddenly, Jade flew over and landed next to her.
"I heard you are sculpting a sculpture for Ruby's party!" She exclaimed.

"Yes I am!"
"Did you know that Sapphire is really good at cloud sculpting? She wants to be a professional cloud sculptor one day."
Diamond felt a cut to her heart but she tried to ignore it."I know."
"Oh... Maybe she could help you?"
"I don't need any help."
Jade stepped back. Suddenly she gasped."What's the matter?" Diamond asked.
"Your stone!"
Diamond looked down at her stone and noticed that it was slowly turning black.

"What happened to my stone?!" Diamond gasped.
"I'm not sure... we should ask Topaz. She pretty much knows everything about anything. And if she doesn't know, she'll find out."
"But I have to finish my sculpture!"
"Are you sure you don't want to let Sapphire do it? I know she would really love it and that way we could take care of your stone."
"No, I don't want Sapphire to do it, I want to do it!" Diamond raised her voice.
Jade stepped back.
"Suit yourself." She frowned. "I'll talk to Topaz myself."

Jade rushed to find Topaz. She soon found her in Garden Square, setting up the drink station.

"Topaz, I have to ask you a question!" Jade gasped for air.

"Jade, I really don't have time for-" Topaz started.

"It's Diamond! Her stone turned black!"

"Black?"

"Do you know why?"

"No... but we're going to find out."

"I just can't get it right!" Diamond sighed while trying to sculpt a cloud.
"What are you doing?" A faint voice asked. Diamond whirled around and saw Sapphire.
"Sapphire! Hi! I was just... I'm just sculpting a cloud for Ruby's party."
"Wow. I can't wait to see it finished. I didn't know you sculpted too.
What happened to your stone?"
"I don't know. It just slowly turned black... I don't know why."
"Maybe it happens when we ignore our gifts. You have love, right? Have you not shown love to someone lately?"
Diamond stopped to think and began to realize that she actually didn't.

"What in the world are you two doing?!" Ruby exclaimed when she saw Jade and Topaz studying a book.

"We just have to research something very important." Topaz answered.

"Important for you, maybe. What about my brother's party?"

"Amber told us that everything is pretty much done and she can finish the last details." Jade commented.

"We just need to figure out something for Diamond really quick."

"Speaking of Diamond, where is that girl with that sculpture? I have to leave to pick up my brother from the landing port and I didn't get to see it yet!" Ruby said anxiously.

"Calm down, Ruby, just go get your brother! I'll make sure Diamond gets here with the sculpture on time."
Amber assured her.
"I was hoping to see it before I left." Ruby sighed. "But even if I don't like it it's too late to turn back now."
"I'm sure it will be fine." Amethyst sighed.
"It will have to be... I need to get going." And with that Ruby flew off.
"I better go find Diamond before Ruby ruffles her feathers." Amber said as she was about to take off.
"Hold on, I think that is her now!" Amethyst said while looking up. Sure enough, Diamond was flying in,
toting a covered cloud sculpture. She landed and placed it right in the middle of the square.
"All finished!" Diamond announced.
"Can we see it?" Jade asked while walking up with Topaz.

"Nope! It's a surprise!" Diamond said excitedly. At that moment Sapphire flew in.
"I hope I'm not too late." She commented. "Diamond said that Ruby is having a welcome home party for her brother."
"She just left to pick him up from the landing port." Amber told her.
"Is that your sculpture?" Sapphire asked Diamond. "Can I see it?"
"It's going to be a surprise." Diamond smiled.
Jade and Topaz looked at each other.
"Look, Jade!" Topaz whispered. "Diamond's stone isn't black anymore!"
"That's strange... but good. We should ask her later what that was all about then."
"Here they come!" Amethyst announced while everyone turned to look up.

"I am proud to announce..." Ruby started while landing. "The homecoming of my very dear big brother... Jasper."

Another red pegasus landed next to Ruby. All the girls began to greet him.

"It's so nice to meet all of you." Jasper smiled as he began walking around. "Is all this for me?"

"Sure is!" Ruby beamed proudly. "Aren't I the best little sister in the world?"

"Of course you are." Jasper hugged her. Then he looked up curiously at the covered sculpture. "What is this?"

"This is a cloud sculpture for you." Diamond smiled while pulling back the blanket. Everyone gasped at the beautiful sculpture... especially Sapphire. It was one of *her* sculptures she made! Did Diamond really steal one from her and try to take credit for it? Sapphire decided not to say anything.
"It's stunning!" Ruby exclaimed.
"I'll say." Jasper commented. "I'll have to mention this in one of my articles."
"Then you're going to have to talk to the artist that made this." Diamond smiled.
"Sapphire!" She called out. "Come over here!"

Sapphire was surprised to hear her name.

"Me?" she asked.

"You did sculpt this cloud, didn't you?" Jasper asked.

"Um… y-yes, I did."

"Do you happen to have any more available?"

"She has tons, don't you Sapphire?" Diamond asked while nudging her. "Most of them are over in Sunset Valley."

"Okay, okay, we can all check out Sapphire's sculptures after food and games. Let's eat everyone!" Ruby announced.

Sapphire walked next to Diamond.

"That was really nice of you to do that for me, Diamond. I know how much you wanted to sculpt a cloud for this party. It means a lot to me. I don't think I would have the courage to do it myself."

"That's not true, Sapphire. Your gift is courage. And I'm sorry I wasn't staying true to mine today. Either way, I'm sure I'm going to find something else to dream about soon." Diamond said and then they both laughed and went to join everyone in the party.

Story Reflections

DIAMOND
Princess Of Love

Being the Princess of Love, Diamond realized that the most powerful love is sacrificial love. Giving up of herself for the benefit of someone else wasn't easy, but it was an act of true love. Jesus sacrificed himself to pay for all the bad things we did so we can be right with God. His sacrifice was the hardest but best sacrifice of all. Sometimes Satan tries to discourage us and have us think selfishly, and we might even get some bad advice from our own friends! The best is to always look to God's word for answers. Jesus also encourages us to look for the benefit of others and to love them as we would love ourselves. Loving others isn't always easy, but by doing so we are using the power of God to fight evil and are spreading Christ's name wherever we go.

Bible Verse:

"(Jesus said) Love one another as I have loved you."

-John 13:34

www.anchristiancomics.com

54.

AMETHYST
Princess Of Faith

3

"Race you to that pole!" A little pagasus called out while zooming through the clouds.
"No fair, you didn't count to three!" Amethyst replied while flying after her. The little pegasus reached the pole and summersaulted excitedly.
"I won!" She exclaimed. "I can't believe you were beaten by your little sister!"
"Now Crystal, don't boast." Amethyst frowned.
"Just kidding sis!" Crystal said, and then she started to cough a little.

"Oh my goodness, are you okay? Do you think you're getting sick?"

"Oh, Amethyst, you worry too much! I'm fine!" Crystal started coughing some more.

"We better get home." Amethyst started to turn her back.

"But we're having so much fun!"

"We'll play some games inside… it will be fun!"

That night, Crystal became very sick. The doctor came to visit and told Amethyst and their father that it was very serious and there was nothing he could do to heal her. Amethyst's father started to cry.
"Don't worry, daddy." Amethyst told him. "Maybe I can visit Prince Morning Star... I'm sure he wouldn't mind since it's urgent. He is the most powerful pegasus ever... I'm sure he has a cure."
Trying not to doubt, Amethyst gathered up her faith and went to see Prince Morning Star.

After getting to the castle, Amethyst explained her situation to the guards. One of them went to find the Prince, and came back with some news.

"Prince Morning Star will not see you at this time." The guard told her. Amethyst's heart sank. Why would Prince Morning Star not see her? Didn't he care about her? Before Amethyst could say any more, the guard spoke up again.

"But I have a message from him." The guard continued. "He said you need to travel to the Land of Flora and find a powerful, rare flower to make a tea out of and give to your sister before it is too late. The flower is called The Scarlet and is red, outlined with gold. You will find it in the deepest part of the Crystal Cave. He says have faith… your sister will be healed."

Amethyst thanked the guard and thought aloud, "I must do this for Crystal. Maybe I could ask Topaz to come with me since she knows so much."
Suddenly a shadowy figure formed as she passed by. Out of the darkness slowly formed a dragon… the Dragon of Chaos! He chuckled as he watched her leave.

"I know what Prince Morning Star is doing. He is trying to strengthen her faith. Well, we'll just have to stop that, now won't we? If Princess Amethyst's sister doesn't get that remedy in time… she will die. And if she dies, that will make Prince Morning Star a liar. And if Prince Morning Star is a liar, then he will never be trusted again." And with that, Chaos disappeared into the darkness.

Topaz happily agreed to accompany Amethyst on her journey. "I've heard of the Land of Flora."
She said while digging through a chest full of maps. "It's a wild land full of plants and caves and
rocks and… here it is." She pulled out a little map and unrolled it. The two looked at it together.
"I think our best bet would be to go through Rainbow Pass and just shy of Sky Haven."
Amethyst sighed. "Don't worry." Topaz assured her. "We'll find that flower."

62.

The two began their journey. Little did they know that Chaos was watching their every move. He sped ahead to one of the crossroad signs and chuckled. "Let's play a little game… shall we?" He said to himself while switching the signs. As the girls were approaching he disappeared. Topaz looked at the sign, confused.

"That's weird. I'm pretty sure Rainbow Pass is the other way." She commented.

"We don't have time!" Amethyst called out desperately while flying ahead. "The sign says Rainbow Pass, so let's go!"

Topaz just shrugged and followed her. Chaos grinned as he watched them from the shadows, proud of his evil trickery.

After Amethyst and Topaz had been flying for hours, Topaz started to get suspicious.
"Amethyst, I don't think…" Suddenly she stopped. "Oh no."
"What is it?" Amethyst asked.
"Over there… that's Nitro City. We've been flying the wrong way!"
"What?!"
"Somebody must have switched the signs!"
"Oh, we're never going to make it in time!" Amethyst started to stress out. Her stone slowly began to turn black.
"Amethyst, stop worrying! Your stone is turning black!"
"What does that mean?"
"That means you're not using your gift, which is faith. We'll just turn back. I wouldn't be surprised if it

was some kind of trick of Chaos to throw us off course. Don't give in!"
Amethyst sighed and the two turned around and flew back to the signs.

There were no more distractions the rest of the way. They flew through Rainbow Pass and passed Sky Haven.
"We're getting close" Topaz encouraged Amethyst. Suddenly they approached a wild looking, plant overrun forest.
"That's it!" Topaz shouted excitedly. "That's the Land of Flora!"
"Do you see where the Crystal Cave might be?" Amethyst asked.
"It says here on the map that the entrance is at the base of the volcano next to a pond."
"I think I see it from here. Let's land!"

Amethyst was thankful that, other than the sign mix-up, everything was going good so far. They landed right next to the pond and there was the entrance to Crystal Cave.

"This seems almost too easy." Amethyst thought aloud.

"Don't be so doubtful. Let's go." Topaz urged as they entered into the cave. Suddenly the ground started rumbling and rocks started falling.

"Look out!" Topaz shouted while pushing Amethyst out of the way.

A rock hit her head and left her unconscious.

"Topaz!" Amethyst shouted. She flew to her and tried to wake her up.

"Please wake up Topaz!"

"I guess it's just you and me." A deep voice whispered in the darkness. Amethyst jumped back. She looked up and saw Chaos standing in front of her.

"Sorry about that little rock slide. But we can't have you leaving this cave, now can we?" He smirked.

"So tell me, Princess Amethyst, do you still have faith that your sister will be healed? Can Morning Star really save her... even though he didn't even want to see you in person?"

"How do you know that?" Amethyst asked.

"I know everything."

Suddenly he slammed his foot against the ground and the whole cave shook. Then the ground stopped shaking and Amethyst looked around. Chaos was gone, and it was quiet. Just then Amethyst heard a sizzling sound. She turned and saw lava slowly oozing out of the cracks in the rocks.
"The volcano!" She gasped. "Topaz you need to wake up right now!" Amethyst tried to wake her friend, but it was no use. She flew to the entrance of the cave and tried to move some of the rocks, but they wouldn't budge.
"We're trapped!" She cried. "I should've never came here! I should've never listened to Morning Star!" Amethyst sunk to the floor, crying. Her stone slowly started to fade until it turned black.

Suddenly Amethyst caught sight of a little glimmer in the corner of her eye. She turned and saw a beautiful flower with gold lining growing out of one of the rocks.

"The Scarlet Flower!" She gasped.

Amethyst's stone slowly started glowing again. She frowned with determination.

"Faith is believing without seeing!" She said as she grabbed the flower and put it into Topaz's sack.

"I don't see a way out, but Morning Star said my sister will be healed so I know somehow we're going to get out of here!"

Amethyst slipped Topaz on her back and looked up at the rocks towering above her, blocking the entrance.
"I will always believe in you Prince Morning Star!" She shouted.
Suddenly a bright light shone from her stone, breaking the rock wall down. Amethyst was astounded!
"Let's get out of here!" she called while flying out, and not a moment too soon. The lava began filling the cave and flowing out. Amethyst took a quick dip in the pond to refresh Topaz and kept on going.
Topaz slowly blinked her eyes open.
"What happened?" she asked.
"Don't worry… you were knocked out, but we got the flower and are on our way home!"

70.

All of a sudden a scaly tail grabbed Topaz and tightly wrapped its coils around her. Amethyst whirled around and saw Chaos tightly squeezing her with his tail. Topaz winced in pain.

"Let her go!" Amethyst yelled.

"Morning Star is a liar." Chaos frowned angrily as he grabbed Topaz's sack and then sped away just as soon as he came.

"The flower was in that sack! We can't get any more because the cave is burned with lava! We have to get it back!" Amethyst said anxiously as she started to fly after Chaos, but Topaz stopped her.

"Let it go, Amethyst. It's too late." Topaz sighed.
"Fine, but I realized something." Amethyst frowned.
"What?"
"No matter what happens, I will never doubt Prince Morning Star. What's the point of faith if you give up right when things don't turn out? And something else... if I don't stay true to Morning Star then there is only one other person to serve... and that is Chaos. Why would I want to please the very one that is making me suffer?"

"You're right." Topaz said. "It's so interesting how he was so nice to us at first just to get us to follow him, but once we rejected him he became the most horrid beast ever to exist."

"I will not let him win. He can have the flower. Somehow, Crystal will be okay. I know because Morning Star said so… and that's all I need to know."

After the tiresome journey, Amethyst and Topaz finally reached Amethyst's house. Amethyst stopped... afraid to go inside.

"It's going to be okay." Topaz assured her.

Amethyst frowned with determination and walked inside. She saw her father standing there as she walked in.

"Daddy... how's Crystal?" She asked.

"We have a visitor." He smiled.
Amethyst looked up and saw Morning Star walking toward them, smiling.
"Prince Morning Star!" Amethyst and Topaz bowed.
"Your sister will be fine. I made the Scarlet tea and served it to her." He told them.
"You had the ingredients all along? Then why did you send me to go find it?" Amethyst asked, confused.

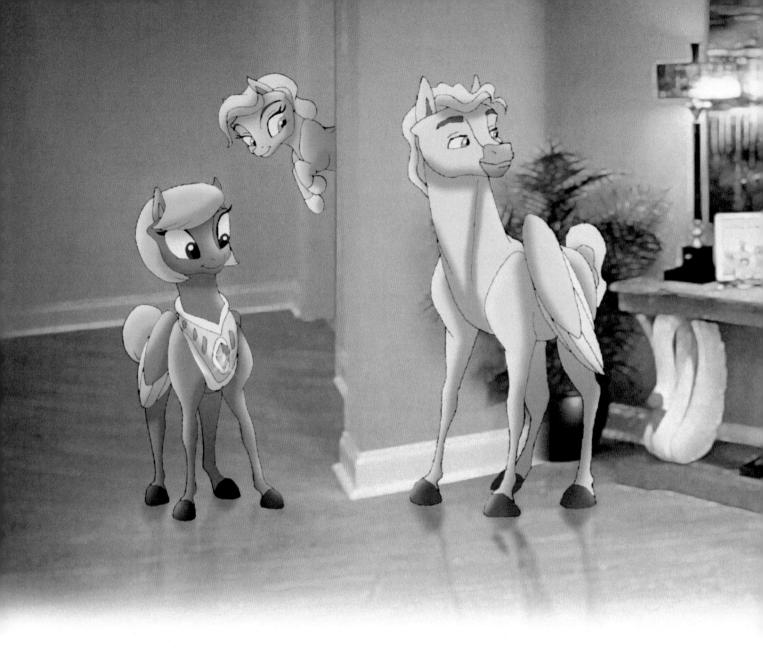

"To strengthen your faith. I know it was hard, but it was what was best for you. Now, because of this experience, in the future your gift will come more naturally. And you will be able to share your experience with others to help give them faith as well." Morning Star answered. "There's always a reason for anything that happens. I will never let you down. Ever. It was wise of you to believe my word."

And with that Morning Star bent down and gave Amethyst a warm hug. Then he said his goodbyes and left. Amethyst stood at the door and watched him go. Crystal snuck out of her room and stood next to Amethyst.

"We really have the best King, don't we?" Crystal asked.

"Yes." Amethyst smiled. "We do. We most certainly do."

Story Reflections
AMETHYST
Princess Of Faith

It was very hard for Amethyst to have faith and believe what Prince Morning Star said because so many things were going wrong. That happens to us too! So many times we ask God to help us and it seems like so many things aren't going our way, and we feel like God doesn't care about us. But He does, and He loves us so much! The Bible says that everything happens for a reason, and whatever is happening to us will glorify God one way or another! Only God can take a bad situation and turn it out for good. The Bible also says that without faith it is impossible to please God… for if we believe that he exists we have to have faith because we can't physically see him. But we know he is there because the things we can see prove that he is there. God is all around us… in nature, in family, in friends… any time anything good happens to you, that's God working through that person! Even though we think we know what we need sometimes but don't get it, we need to have faith that God is the one who really knows what's best for us. Trust him… he knows what he's doing!

Bible Verse:

"But without faith it is impossible to please (God): for he that cometh to God must believe that he is, and that he is a rewarder of them that diligently seek him."

–Hebrews 11:6

AMBER
Princess Of Patience

The Pegasus Princesses all gathered together for an urgent meeting held by Diamond. As everyone settled down, Diamond began to speak.

"I just got a message from Prince Morning Star." Diamond told them. "He wants us all to go and visit a place called Tainment Central. He says that the pegasus there are in real danger and we need to help them."

"Sounds scary." Sapphire cowered.

"Bring it on!" Amber shouted. "Where is this Tainment Central?"

"Supposedly Tainment Central is a very expensive place to live. I hear it looks really nice." Topaz spoke up.

"Did you say 'expensive'? Count me in!" Ruby cheered excitedly.

"Count ALL of us in. Morning Star said all of our stones are needed for this place." Diamond said seriously. "Topaz, will you set the course?"

"Way ahead of you, Diamond!" Topaz smiled while taking off. "Let me take a look at my maps and I'll be right back!"

"Be prepared girls." Diamond told them. "There's no telling what we will find in this place."

Tainment Central ended up not being too far from Friesia. "It should be just over these pink clouds!" Topaz said while glancing at her map.

"Oh my, I have never been so excited in my whole life! I know I will blend right in with these rich people!" Ruby smiled.

"I'm sure you will." Amber said under her breath. "I don't have the patience to deal with a thousand Rubys that have money."

"Um… is it supposed to look that way?" Sapphire asked.

Everyone looked and saw the city was dark, deserted, and forgotten. The girls landed and cautiously looked around.

"What happened to this place?" Diamond asked.

"We can explore the shops first… just in case we find a rich souvenir or something." Ruby suggested.

"Sh! I hear something!" Diamond whispered. They all listened and heard faint sounds. "This way!"

The girls came to the edge of the city and were surprised at what they saw. There were tons of pegasus standing together... although they didn't seem like they even knew that they were together. All of them were standing on their own platforms with shackles clamped around their legs and dark goggles strapped around their eyes. They were moving around in strange ways and making strange noises... some of them were even talking to themselves.

84.

"Ugh, who are these creepies? It smells like they haven't bathed in months!" Ruby covered her nose.
"You guys… I think these are the citizens of Tainment Central." Diamond said.
"What's happened to them? What are they doing?" Amethyst asked aloud.
"Let's find out!" Amber said while zooming into one of the pegasus and knocking him off of his platform.

"Ugh, WHO DID THAT?!" He angrily yelled while ripping his goggles off. He looked up and saw Amber. "What in the world is that and why are you all just moving around on platforms like dummies?!" Amber asked harshly.

"Amber, not so hard." Amethyst frowned.

"Don't tell me you never heard of Virtual Reality!" The Pegasus laughed. All the girls were quiet. "Wow, where are you from? Some hillbilly town?"

"Don't dis us! You're the ones that look ridiculous!" Amber shouted.

"Calm down Amber!" Diamond frowned.

"Virtual Reality is amazing. All you need to do is stand on the platform and wear the goggles. You can access the programming and choose any world you want to be in… or make up your own. You can play all kind of games and be anything you want to be. With the goggles on, it really looks like you're in this make believe world. It's so cool! It's so addictive, you'll never want to come back to the real world ever again!" He explained."Here, try it!"
He strapped the goggles on Amber and pushed her onto the platform.

Inside the goggles, Amber saw the words asking "Where would you like to be? Just imagine it and say 'enter'".

"Enter!" Amber said aloud.

The girls just looked at each other. Suddenly Amber jumped above the platform and started flapping and jumping and twisting.

"I wonder what she's seeing." Topaz thought aloud.

Suddenly Amber ripped off the goggles and jumped off of the platform.

"That was so cool!" She shouted. "I was flying through a storm and dodging all these lightning bolts while escaping giant mosquitos! It felt like it was happening in real life!"

"Out of all the things you could pick, you chose to do that?!" Ruby wailed.

"See, I told you it's amazing, you could get one for yourself, it only costs…" the pegasus started, but stopped as Amber threw the goggles, hitting him on the head.

"Don't you see? It's dangerous because it is amazing. Virtual reality is fine, but not when you live in it instead of the real world. Everyone's so busy living in these fake worlds, they don't even know what the real world is anymore. Look what happened to your town! Look at everyone... no families, friends, nothing! They're so busy in this virtual reality junk they dumped them. And look at you! Dirty, smelly... and when do you even have time to eat? Do you eat virtual food too?!" Amber shouted impatiently. Her stone slowly started to turn black.

"Amber, your stone is turning black! That happened to me before!" Amethyst called out after she noticed. "That's a sign that you're not using your gift! Be patient!"

"If you MUST know, we do eat. Our food is delivered to us by Alabaster." The pegasus frowned.

"Who's Alabaster?" Diamond asked.

Just then, a white and orange Pegasus came through with a cart of food and started handing out their orders.

"Opal, you ordered a pizza pie? Peridot, your chicken fingers…"

Alabaster said while delivering the food.

91.

"This is beyond weird!" Amber cried in frustration.

"If you don't like it, then leave!" The pegasus said while jumping back on his platform. "I'm Onyx, by the way. In case you were wondering… you didn't even care to ask. Just jumped right into your business."
And with that he put his goggles back on and ignored them.

"Fine! We'll leave!" Amber stomped.

"We can't leave, Amber." Diamond told her.

"We tried our best, there's nothing we can do."

"We need to be patient in these kind of situations. You can't expect someone to change right away."

"Ugh!" Amber groaned. "I'm just not a patient person! It's not who I am!"

"Morning Star doesn't think so."

"I guess. Whatever, let's go confront this Alabaster guy!"

The gang walked up to Alabaster. "Hi there! We're from out of town, and we were wondering if you could tell us about-" Diamond started, but Alabaster cut her off.
"Yes, I can tell. Leave these poor people alone. They don't want your help." He sneered.
"Excuse me!" Ruby huffed. "That is no way to treat guests!"
"Guests?! More like invaders! If you want a Virtual Reality set, by all means, stay. If not, leave."
"And where are these Virtual Reality sets coming from?" Diamond asked, suspiciously.
"If you don't want one, you don't need to know." Alabster said as he turned around and kept passing out food. "My job is to keep these people satisfied... not answer questions."

93.

"But they can't be satisfied if they don't even live in the real world! Especially if they know nothing about Morning Star!" Diamond called after him.

"I DON'T WORK FOR MORNING STAR!" Alabaster angrily whirled around. Smoke was coming out of his nostrils and his eyes started to glow green.

"No, you don't." Diamond frowned. "And there's only one other person you can be working for."

Alabaster angrily spit fire at them. They all rushed to take cover.

"This is crazy!" Amber frowned. "This is all just a trick of Chaos! He wants these people to live in a fake world so they can't follow Morning Star in this one!"

"What do we do?" Sapphire asked.

"Go home! These pegasus belong to Chaos! See their shackles? They are virtually bound!" Alabaster shouted. He turned and spit fire toward Diamond. She jumped and accidentally knocked one of the other pesgasus over. The pegasus got up and shook her head. Her goggles had fallen off and she blinked as she looked up. When she saw Alabaster spitting fire, she gasped.

"Alabaster?" She asked, surprised.

"Get down!" Amber shouted while pushing her away as more fire was spit.

"My name is Moonstone. What's going on?" She asked.

"Alabaster is working for an evil dragon named Chaos. He's the one that made this virtual reality junk to keep you from living in the real world. He doesn't want you guys to know about the true King." Amber told her.

"We have a king?"

Amber pushed her out of the way again to avoid the fire.

"I can't believe I was living in Virtual Reality so long." Moonstone said sadly.

"It's not too late to change it." Amber told her. "You need to help us."

Moonstone nodded. "I know just what to do. There's a switch that will turn off the Virtual Reality machine. I'll turn it off, and then everyone will have to open their eyes to what is going on." Moonstone began going around turning off all of the machines. The pegasus were confused at first, but gasped when they saw Alabaster attacking with fire.

"Put your goggles back on, now!" He shouted furiously. As Moonstone turned off Onyx's machine, he jumped off of his platform angrily.

"Leave me alone!" He yelled.

"Onyx, look what's happening!" Moonstone told him. Onyx looked and saw Alabaster fighting the princesses.

"I don't care." He huffed while turning his machine back on. "As long as I'm in my own world, it doesn't matter."

"Is this guy for real?!" Amber shouted angrily, her stone turning more black by the minute.

"Amber, your stone! Be careful!" Diamond called out. "We can't defeat Alabaster without you!"

Each girl started talking to everyone individually.

"You have to have faith in what Prince Morning Star sent us to tell you." Amethyst told one.

"You can't love your friends, family, others, or even get love back if you live in a fake world." Diamond told another.

"Living in a world where you're the best and everything goes the way you want it is actually destroying you!" Ruby said to one.

"It's not easy, but you have to take courage and face what's going on in the real world." Sapphire told one.

"You don't deserve Morning Star caring enough to save you, but because of his mercy real life is way better than this machine and actually has a purpose." Topaz said to another.

"Don't be sad that you have to leave your fun world, be happy that you are not lost in it anymore." Jade encouraged one.

As each girl talked to the other pegasus, their stones lit up. Amber looked down at hers and saw it was still black. She sighed and lay down next to Onyx's platform... not saying a word.

Amber's stone quickly lit up, and the princesses' light combined and blinded Alabaster. Alabaster shielded his eyes from the light and flew away. All of a sudden the shackles fell off of all of the pegasus… except Onyx. The crowd cheered.

"Thank you so much for coming here!" One of the pegasus thanked the princesses.

"It's not going to be easy, but we'll help you rebuild your city." Diamond told them.

"And while we do, we'll tell you all about Prince Morning Star!" Jade exclaimed. Everyone happily started making their way back into the city. Amber was now left alone with Onyx. She just sat there and waited… not saying a word. After a few hours, the sun started to go down. Onyx suddenly stopped moving and slowly removed his goggles. He looked around and saw everyone was gone… except Amber.

"You're still here?" He asked. "Why are you waiting here so long?"

"Because you are important to Prince Morning Star." Amber told him. "And I'm not leaving you because I know how dangerous this virtual machine is."

"You care that much?"

"Yes."

"I can't leave my world." Onyx sighed.

"Fine." Amber frowned, not budging. It was quiet. Suddenly Onyx's goggles fell to the ground. Amber looked up.

"I know you're right." Onyx said softly. "It's just so much better in my world."

"A world without Prince Morning Star isn't worth living in." Amber smiled.

Onyx smiled back at her, and his shackles slowly fell off. The two made their way back into the city, leaving the shackles behind.

Story Reflections
AMBER
Princess Of Patience

Patience is something that is very hard for most people to have. Most of the time we don't feel like waiting for things to happen... we want things now! Like Amber in the story, sometimes it's very hard to be patient with people. Maybe you know someone like Onyx, who you know is making bad choices and you are trying to show them otherwise but they just don't listen and keep living the way they want. It's so hard to be patient when we pray for someone like this day after day and don't see any change. But God has the power to turn any situation around and the Bible says his timing is perfect! Many times it's better for certain things not to happen right away because patience is needed to be learned. Don't give up on hard situations and especially don't give up on praying... just be patient and wait on the Lord. He will always come through.

Bible Verse:

"And not only so, but we glory in tribulations also: knowing that tribulation worketh patience; And patience, experience; and experience, hope:"
Romans 5: 3-4

Pegasus™ Princesses
PARABLES FOR KIDS

www.anchristiancomics.com

RUBY
Princess Of Humbleness

5

"Oh yeah, I look good!" Ruby commented while looking at herself in the mirror.
"I think you have a pretty good chance at winning this beauty contest, Ruby." Sapphire commented while hanging up clothes that Ruby threw on floor while she was trying to decide what to wear.
"A good chance? It's not even a question that I'm going to win. They should skip the contest and just give me the award... it would save them money and time. Do you know what the grand prize is? An all-inclusive trip to Fashion Island for two! I've always wanted to go there!"

"That sounds like fun. I like it at home, though." Sapphire commented.

"You would, Sapphire. Thanks for helping me with a second opinion. I can always count on you to give me compliments." Ruby flung her hair.

"I'm glad I could be useful."

"Oh my, look at the time! We better get going! All the contestants must be there an hour early!" And with that, Ruby grabbed Sapphire and they flew out the door.

Meanwhile, the rest of the Pegasus Princesses were making their way to the competition.
"I'm so not looking forward to Ruby trying to show off to the whole village." Amber sighed. "Do we really have to go?"
"Come on, Amber, Ruby is our friend. We have to support her." Diamond told her.
"She doesn't need support, she's so full of it she can support herself."
Amethyst chuckled at the comment.
"We need to be there for each other. Even Sapphire went to her house to help her get ready for the contest." Diamond commented.
"The only reason she probably asked Sapphire to help is because Sapphire is too afraid to say anything but nice things." Amber frowned.

There ended up being a lot of people in the crowd who came to watch the beauty contest. Ruby waited behind the curtains, excited. She impatiently watched the different pegasus walk up and down the stage, waiting for her turn.

"This is my competition? You can't even compare!" Ruby sneered.

Finally, her name was called out and Ruby proudly walked up and down the stage. Her friends cheered for her... except Amber closed her eyes.

"This is so embarrassing." She groaned. But there was also another person very interested in Ruby... one of Chaos' minions disguised as a pegasus. He quietly watched among the crowd waiting for the right chance.

The time came for the judges to make a decision. One of the judges stood up and announced: "And the winner of the Friesia Pegasus Beauty Pageant is…"

"This is it!" Ruby stomped excitedly behind the stage. She decided to jump out on the stage as the judge announced her name.

"Rose Quartz!" The judge finished.

Ruby jumped out on the stage and yelled "That's me! Thank you, thank you!"

Everyone was silent and just stared at her. Amber slapped her forehead in frustration.

"Um, excuse me?" A faint voice asked.

Ruby turned and saw another contestant walking from behind the curtain behind her.

"*I'm* Rose Quartz."

108.

"Wait, what?" Ruby turned to look at everyone.

She realized it wasn't her name that was announced. Suddenly, in the silence, somebody stifled a grin.

Then one person started chuckling... then another... and soon the whole crowd was laughing at Ruby.

"But, but... this is just not fair!" Ruby sobbed as she took off.

"Ruby, come back!" Diamond yelled after her.

She heard some chuckling next to her and saw it was Amber.

"Amber!"

"Sorry. She had it coming for her, though."

"Let's go try to find her." Diamond sighed.

Ruby found a little bridge to be alone and cry under. "This is the most embarrassing day of my life!" She wailed.

"Excuse me?" A voice asked. Ruby whirled around and saw a handsome pegasus standing there. She didn't know, but it was actually Chaos' minion in disguise.

"Oh, hello." Ruby said, quickly trying to fix herself up.

"I just came from the beauty contest and I wanted to find you to make sure you are okay."

"Oh, how kind. Have we met?"

"Not yet. My name is Jonquil. I just wanted to find you and tell you that I think you are the most beautiful pegasus I've ever seen, and I know you deserved that award."

"I wish you were one of the judges." Ruby sniffed.

"Do you want to know what I think?" He whispered. "I think this contest was rigged. There is no way someone like Rose Quartz could win this contest over you."

"You're quite right! I mean, who is this Rose Quartz?! I deserve to go to Fashion Island!" Ruby agreed.

As her pride began to build, her stone slowly began to fade. Jonquil noticed and smirked happily, knowing that he was slowly ruining the gift of humbleness that Prince Morning Star had given her.

"Someone as beautiful as you should not have to suffer like this. And you know you are beautiful because if a stranger like me came all the way to find you and tell you, it must be true." He continued. "Well, it appears I am the laughing stock of all of Friesia." Ruby huffed.

"You don't have to be. You show Rose Quartz. I can help if you want. We will embarrass her so much no one will even remember your little slip up on the stage. And I promise you I'll get you that trip to Fashion Island."

"Really?" Ruby asked excitedly.

"Ruby!" A voice called from the distance. Ruby looked up and saw her friends flying toward her. She looked back at Jonquil and saw that he was gone.

"Who was that?" Amber asked.

"Someone with taste." Ruby said, holding her head high.

"We wanted to see if you were okay." Diamond said gently.

"Oh, I am quite fine. Never better. Actually, I'm a bit tired. I'm going home." And with that, Ruby flew off into the clouds.

"Something's fishy here. Who was that guy and what did he tell her?" Amber frowned. "I'm going to go spy on her!"

"Amber! You're horrid!" Amethyst gasped. "Spying on your own friend?"

"Well, something's not right... someone's got to find out what's going on." Amber blurted as she took off after Ruby.

Ruby got home and began to plot on how she would disgrace Rose Quartz.

"I wish Jonquil was here!" She sighed. Suddenly there was a knock at her window. Low and behold, there he was!

"What are you doing here?" She asked excitedly.

"I followed you. I wanted to help you with our plan against Rose Quartz!"

"Oh, you are wonderful! Come in!"

"Actually, I'd like to show you my idea. Follow me."

Ruby excitedly followed him out the window. Amber watched them in the distance.

"What are they up to?" She asked aloud.

115.

Ruby and Jonquil ended up at the empty stage that was used for the contest.

"What are we doing here?" Ruby asked.

"We're going to prove that Rose Quartz rigged this contest, and YOU deserve to be the winner."
He answered.

"But how? I don't even know if it was even her who rigged it."

"It doesn't matter... we need to embarrass her, don't we? Take this camera."

Jonquil handed her a video camera.

"Now, I'll act out Rose Quartz slipping her name in the winner envelope and switching it with yours.
Film me." He ordered.

"Film you? But how..."

Suddenly Jonquil transformed into Rose Quartz.

"How did you do that?" She gasped.

"Doesn't matter, just film! We're wasting time!"

Ruby started to film Jonquil disguised as Rose Quartz cheating for the contest. Suddenly, she stopped.

"I can't do this." Ruby sighed. "It does not feel right to frame Rose Quartz for something she didn't do."

"She's the one that's ruining your life. We just need proof of something that probably already happened and you'll get the award for the contest. Isn't that what you deserve?" Jonquil asked.

"Well, yes, but…"

Suddenly Amber flew in and landed in between Ruby and Jonquil. Jonquil quickly formed back into himself.

117.

"I've been following you and I know what you're up to!" Amber frowned.

"You've been spying on me?!" Ruby gasped angrily.

"It's a good thing I did! Ruby, who in the world is this guy? Why are you listening to him? Doesn't any of this sound suspicious? And you…" Amber turned toward Jonquil. "I have a gut feeling I know who you're working for."

"What are you talking about Amber?" Ruby frowned.

"Take a look at your stone. Black. It wasn't black at the beauty contest, and now it is. After you met this… whatever you are." Amber said looking back at Jonquil.

"I am deeply offended. All I care about is Ruby." Jonquil defended.

"I'm sure you do. You care about losing her gift! Go away!" Amber stomped.

"Ruby, are you going to let her talk to me like this? What has she ever done to help you in your life? All she has ever done is talk you down and belittle you. She even laughed when you were embarrassed on stage." Jonquil said.

"You... laughed, Amber?" Ruby asked, tears in her eyes.

"Who are you going to believe, Ruby? Some jealous little pegasus who doesn't care about you, or me? The one who is trying everything to give you what you always wanted? You choose."

Ruby was quiet and then softly said, "I want to please Morning Star." She looked at her blackened stone. "I may not be very humble, but I know he gave me this stone for a reason. Amber is right." She looked up at Jonquil and frowned. "You're the one that wants to destroy me! I see what you are doing now! You're trying to play with my pride!"

"How dare you accuse me of going against you!" Jonquil shouted angrily.

Suddenly Ruby's stone started to glow. She stood next to Amber's side.

"Amber may be brutal, but at least her power is from the King. Where did you get yours? Not everyone can morph into anything they want. And knowing that Prince Morning Star would never want me to cheat and lie, there's only one other person you can be working for!"

"You will be sorry!" Jonquil angrily formed into one of Chaos' hideous minions.

"No, you will be! I lost that contest fair and square! Time to stop making a big deal out of it and leave Rose Quartz alone!"

Ruby's stone burst with light and a beam shone toward the minion. The light stung him and he yelled in pain and flew away.

It was quiet. Ruby just sighed and looked sadly at the ground.
"Well, this is it. I have the gift of humbleness... so I am destined to be depressed forever. I am nothing, and I can't do anything right. I am worthless."
"You drama queen, being humble doesn't mean to think you're worthless!" Amber frowned.
"Then how else can you be humble?!" Ruby shouted, frustrated.

"Ruby, Prince Morning Star picked you out of all the other pegasus to carry the stone of humbleness. You are strong, confident, and yes, you are beautiful too. You mean a lot to your friends, and you are special. But being humble doesn't mean you aren't those things. Humbleness is knowing that you are, but not because of yourself, but because of Prince Morning Star and the King. They're the ones that made you that way, and it's the power they gave you that will keep you going. Just being thankful for what you are but giving the King the glory is what humbleness really is."

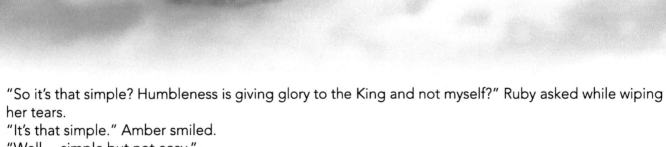

"So it's that simple? Humbleness is giving glory to the King and not myself?" Ruby asked while wiping her tears.

"It's that simple." Amber smiled.

"Well… simple but not easy."

"You know Prince Morning Star would never want you to feel depressed. He loves all of so much. That's why he adopted us as his princesses."

"Bah! I have so much to work on with this whole humbleness issue!" Ruby sobbed while hugging Amber.

"You're such a good friend Amber! You always tell the truth even though it usually hurts! I'm sorrrry!!!!"

"Calm down, Ruby, you're not going to die. I forgive you." She said while gently pushing her away.

"I have an idea. Let's go find the others and plan a trip to Fashion Island together."

"That is the best idea you ever had!" Ruby said excitedly.

"Come on, let's go! I know exactly what to wear!"

"Oh no, what did I start?" Amber sighed as Ruby grabbed her and rushed off into the clouds.

Story Reflections
RUBY
Princess Of Humbleness

Many times it's not easy to be humble... especially when things don't seem fair. Being humble means to not think of ourselves better than other people. Ruby struggled with thinking too highly of herself, and that is exactly why Prince Morning Star gave her the gift of humbleness. Sometimes God gives us gifts to work on that doesn't come naturally so we can strengthen our spirit even more. But we need to be careful because Satan is always there to try to make us lift ourselves up... which is exactly what he did before he got thrown out of heaven! God says he hates pride, which means pride is a very serious sin. But being humble doesn't mean to think of ourselves as being a terrible person... but to give God the glory for all that we are and all that he can make us to be! God doesn't want us to be sad about ourselves but to rejoice because through him we can do anything or be anything he wants us to be! We just need to remember that it's God that is doing the work and not ourselves.

Bible Verse:
"Humble yourselves in the sight of the Lord, and he shall lift
you up."
-James 4:10

SAPPHIRE
Princess Of Courage

Sapphire waited uneasily in the castle gardens. Prince Morning Star had summoned her for a private meeting, and she didn't know what to expect. Soon Morning Star came walking down the garden path toward her. She reverently bowed as he approached.

"Good morning Princess Sapphire." He smiled warmly. "I called you here because I have a very important job for you."

Sapphire nodded shyly, waiting to hear what he had to say.

"There is someone who desperately needs help. He is trapped in a dark land all alone and needs to be saved. I want you to go and find him and bring him back here. His name is Griffith." Suddenly a map formed out of clouds. "You will find him beyond Sugar Cane Mountains, through Hawk Forest and over Redwater Falls. It's far, but don't forget you have my power contained in that stone."

Sapphire looked down at the stone in her breastplate and then back up at Morning Star. "May I take someone with me?" She asked softly.

"I'm afraid not." Prince Morning Star told her. "This situation is very delicate and having more than one pegasus come to Griffith might turn him away from hearing what you have to say. I know you can do this. As long as you keep your stone that I gave you alive, I will always be with you. And with me you will never fail."

130.

Sapphire sighed as she made her way to go find Griffith. Doubts started flooding her mind right away. She was just a little pegasus... what could she do? Who knows what kind of danger Griffith might be in? Would she even have the courage to save him from a scary place? "I have to do this." Sapphire thought aloud. "Scary or not scary, courage is my gift."

Sapphire pressed on and after a while she reached Sugar Cane Mountains. "This part of the journey is nice." She thought. Sugar Cane Mountains were purple cloud peaks with white tips, looking almost as if the tops were sprinkled with sugar. She flew over the mountains like a breeze, but stopped when she came to the entrance of Hawk Forest.

Uneasy, Sapphire slowly made her way into the dark forest. As she looked up the tall, dark trees she saw hundreds of hawks looking down at her. She gasped. They all began to whisper to each other. Sapphire tried to ignore them and kept walking.

Suddenly a hawk swooped down and landed on a trunk in front of her. She let out a scared little yelp.
"Where are you off to, little pegasus? You seem like you're far from home." He asked with a crackly voice.
"I-I'm going past Redwood Falls to save someone called Griffith." She stuttered.
Suddenly the whole forest started laughing.
"Griffith, you say? My, my, little one, that is a pretty tall order. And why would someone like you care for someone like Griffith?"
"Well, I've never met him. But Prince Morning Star sent me to find him." Suddenly the hawks became serious.

134.

"Morning Star?" The hawk asked. "We hawks respect Prince Morning Star."
All the hawks nodded in unison.
"I'm not sure why he would send someone like you to find Griffith, but knowing the Prince, he tends to choose those who seem unworthy to carry out tasks for him. I can lead you as far as Redwood Falls, but you are on your own after that." He told her.
"Would you?" Sapphire asked excitedly. "That would help so much!"

Sapphire soon took off after the hawk as he led her through the forest and over to Redwood Falls. The two landed at the base of the falls and looked up at the water cascading down the rocks.
"I'm afraid you'll have to go the rest of the way alone." He told her.
"Thank you so much. I will make sure to tell Prince Morning Star of your kindness." Sapphire smiled.

136.

As she began to fly up the falls, the hawk called out, "You're very courageous, little one!" Sapphire turned back at him and nodded. He nodded back and then took off toward Hawk Forest. Taking a deep breath, Sapphire continued up the falls. She had no idea what she would find at the top.

As Sapphire flew over the top of the falls, she gasped at what she saw in the distance. Past the water were the darkest clouds she had ever seen, with lightning flashing left and right. She gulped as she slowly made her way toward the dark clouds.

After flying a bit through the dark clouds, Sapphire heard loud slashes and laughing. She peered over one of the clouds and saw an enormous griffon creating storm clouds and sending them off with a mighty blow. Terrified, she ducked back behind the cloud and held her breath.

"I need to find Griffith fast!" She whispered. "Before that griffon finds out that I'm here!"

As she was flying away, she bumped into something. Sapphire shook her head and looked. Standing in front of her was the big, scary griffon! She shrieked with fear.

"Why hello. And what might you be?" He asked while grabbing her.

"I-I'm Princess Sapphire and I've been sent to save someone called Griffith!" She said quickly while shutting her eyes. "Please don't eat me!"

Her stone slowly started to fade for lack of courage.

"*I am* Griffith." The griffon sneered. Sapphire looked up in disbelief.

"WHO SENT YOU?!" He roared.

"Um, um... Prince Morning Star." She whimpered.

"Morning Star?" He said sternly while straightening up. "I was warned about him. He wants to take my power away!"

"What?" Sapphire asked, confused.

"I am ordered to destroy anything and anyone that has to do with Prince Morning Star!" He squeezed Sapphire, but then he stopped.

"Aw, but you are kinda cute, Little Blue. I think I'll keep you. I've been ever so lonely. You can sing to me." Griffith created a cage out of some clouds and stuffed Sapphire inside.

"You can sing, right? Sing to me while I work." He said while making storm clouds.
Sapphire took a closer look and noticed he was wearing a breastplate with a stone… the same
kind Chaos had tried to trick the Pegasus Princesses into wearing some time ago. Around his
wrist he was also wearing gold shackles.
"Where did you get that breastplate?" She asked.

"Some guy named Chaos. He's the one that gave me all this power to do whatever I please.
I make storms and send them over to different cities. He told me that Prince Morning Star is a
threat to taking all my power away." He answered.
"That's not true. Prince Morning Star gave me power." Sapphire told him.
"Yes... power to do something you obviously don't want to do. Chaos gave me power to do
whatever I want to do. And I want to make storms. That's the difference. I'm free."
"Then why do you have shackles around your wrists?"

Griffith looked down and his shackles and thought a bit. Suddenly a huge dragon flew in from beyond the storm. It was Chaos!

"Griffith, I need you to send a typhoon over to Rustnut Village." Chaos ordered.

"But, I was just making a…" Griffith started.

"Excuse me?" Chaos asked. "You never talk back to me. I say 'jump', you say 'how high?' What's this?" Chaos looked at Sapphire in the cage.

"You traitor! I told you to destroy anything that has to do with Prince Morning Star!" He growled.

"But Little Blue would never even hurt a little fly. And I'm kind of lonely up here…"

"Don't talk about being lonely when I gave you everything you ever wanted!"

And with that, Chaos grabbed Sapphire's cage and started to fly away.

144.

"Wait! She's mine!" Giffith called out. He flew after Chaos and tried to grab her back, but suddenly Chaos' shackles lit up and attached to Griffith's.

"Have you ever wondered why you are wearing shackles, Griffith? It's because you belong to me." He threw Griffith back to the ground.

Sapphire tried to squeeze out of the cage bars. Her stone slowly started to turn black with fear.

"You will never be aloud to leave this island without my say so! And I will not allow you to be a friend of a princess of the King! She will spoil everything I have made you to become!" He yelled.

"Well I don't want your power anymore if that's what comes with it!" Griffith told him.

"Well it's too late! You're mine, and no one can ever save you from me!"

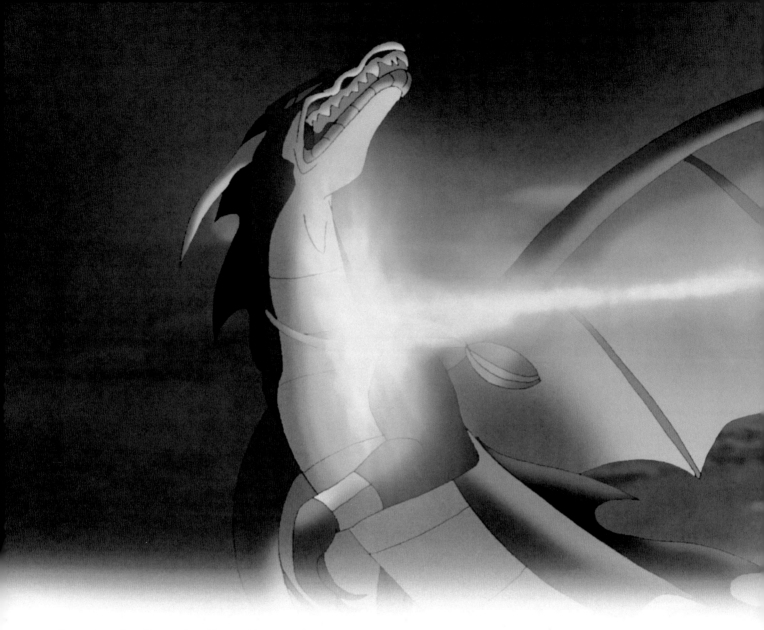

Sapphire finally pushed herself through the cage bars and started to fly away. Then she stopped. Did Chaos say "save"? This is what Prince Morning Star was talking about! Griffith needed to be saved from himself and his deal with Chaos!

"Please give me courage, Prince Morning Star!" She whispered aloud.

Her stone slowly started to light back up again. She frowned with determination and flew straight toward Chaos.

"That's not true!" She said boldly. "It is not too late for Griffith! Prince Morning Star wants to take him into his kingdom and free him from this tricky deal you have put him in! Griffith still has a choice! He can give up the power you gave him and trade it for the power of the King!" Sapphire started flying right toward Chaos as fast as she could, ready to fight. Suddenly an enormous beam burst from her stone and the light sent Chaos flying far into the distance. All was quiet, and then Griffith slowly flew up to her.

"You did all this... for me? And can Morning Star really free me from this prison?" Griffith asked.
"If he could give someone like me the gift of courage, he can do anything. The question is, are you ready to serve him and forget about Chaos' promises?"
Griffith looked down at his stone and sighed.
"Will it hurt? To try to leave my power behind?" He asked.
"Maybe a little. I can help you."
Griffith nodded. Sapphire gently flew up to him. Light shone from her stone and into his. It slowly got more and more intense. Griffith winced in pain, and suddenly his stone burst. Sapphire then quietly unlatched his breastplate and it fell to the floor, along with the shackles around his wrists.

Then Sapphire held Griffith's paw as she smiled and said, "Let's go home."
"Thanks, Little Blue." Griffith smiled. Suddenly he grabbed her and threw her on his back. "You're riding this time! You already have been flying enough... hang on!"
Suddenly Griffith sped off and Sapphire held on as tight as she could.
"I'm free! I'm free! Whoo hoo!" He cheered.
As they flew above Hawk Forest, one of the hawks looked up and smiled.
"Well... I'll be." He said, surprised but pleased as he watched
Griffith and Sapphire speed off into the sunset.

Story Reflections
SAPPHIRE
Princess Of Courage

Sometimes we think of courage meaning to not be afraid… but that is not what courage is at all! Courage means to do something that you are afraid of, even though you are afraid while doing it. Sometimes God calls us to do things that we might be afraid to do, and we think we can't do it because we don't have enough courage. But God will give us the courage when we need it. The Bible says when we are weak we are actually strong! The thing is, when we are weak then God can work in us and his name will be glorified even more because everyone knows that people like us wouldn't be able to do certain things without the power of God! Even though Sapphire was afraid of the task that Prince Morning Star gave her, she was still obedient and listened to him. All we need is to be willing to listen to God and he will give us power to carry out the task. It's not about us but about him! And when we handle life that way, there's no telling how many souls we can win for Christ.

Bible Verse:
"Be strong and of a good courage; be not afraid, neither be thou dismayed: for the LORD your God is with you wherever you go."
–Joshua 1:9

TOPAZ
Princess Of Mercy

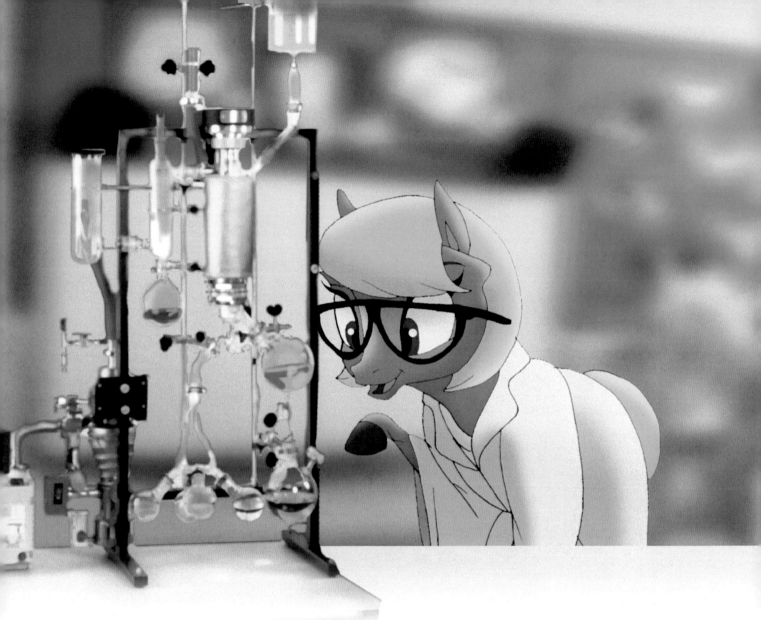

"Oh, this is so nice of you to help me with this Coral!" Topaz said while mixing a solution together in a glass bottle.

"My pleasure Topaz!" Coral said. "I've always been a fan of science but I know I could never be as good as you. So what are you creating again, exactly?"

"A formula that will cause a special paint to light up! It's going to be a shoe-in for the science fair tomorrow!" Topaz said excitedly while taking off her goggles. "This will be the invention of the year!"

"I'll say." Coral smiled. "I'd love to paint myself with paint that lights up! Do you know how cool parties we could have with that?"

"Not only parties, but it will really help safety issues we have when flying in the dark." Topaz put on her goggles and mixed the last ingredient. "Time to test the formula!"

Topaz brushed some of the paint on a small teddy bear.

"The moment of truth! Coral, the lights!" Topaz said.

Coral turned off the lights and suddenly the bear started glowing.

"It's glowing!" Coral exclaimed excitedly.

"It is glowing!" Topaz exclaimed.

They both pranced around excitedly.

"I've been working on this for years! I can't believe it finally works!"

"Okay, you need to create a bunch of different colors, have a bunch of different models and... oh, we're going to make sure your corner looks amazing at the fair! I would be even willing to model some of this paint! I can come up with a little speech for you and everything!" Coral said excitedly.

"Aw, Coral, you're such a good friend. I'm the one who should be supporting and helping you since you're new here to Friesia." Topaz told her.

"By you letting me watch you, that's great." Coral assured her.

"Now let's get cracking! We only got 12 more hours before we need to leave to the science fair!"

Topaz and Coral got to work creating many different varieties of Topaz's new glowing paint.

Deep into the night, though, the girls began to get tired.

"You go rest, Topaz. I can finish cleaning up. You need your strength to present this stuff at the fair tomorrow." Coral told her.

"You're right, but I feel bad for you." Topaz yawned.

"Don't be! I'm too excited to sleep anyways!"

"Thanks so much! You're such a great friend! I can't wait until you meet my other friends."

"Me too. Now go to sleep!"

Topaz nodded and went up the stairs to her room.

That morning, Topaz's alarm rang. She jumped out of bed.
"This is the day!" She exclaimed. "Science fair, here I come!" Topaz rushed down to the basement and flung the door open. "Alright Coral, I'm ready to…" Suddenly Topaz froze. Coral was gone… and so was all of her glowing paint!
"No, no, no, no!" Topaz yelled frantically while searching through her stuff. "They can't be gone!"
Suddenly there was a knock at the door and Jade walked in.

"Hi Topaz! The girls and I wanted to wish you luck and see you off to the science… w-what are you doing?" Jade asked.

"My formula! My inventions! Everything I prepared for the science fair is gone!" Topaz said while grabbing Jade and shaking her in frustration.

"Yeah… that sounds bad. When was the last time you saw them?"

"Last night! Right here! I left them with Coral and… Coral!"

"Who?"

"She's the new girl in town. We became quick friends and she offered to help me with the fair. She MUST know where my stuff is!"

Topaz walked outside with Jade and the other Pegasus Princesses were there cheering for her.

158.

"Stop! I have nothing to cheer for!" Topaz frowned.

"Well... I didn't get enough beauty sleep for this?" Ruby sighed. "You're welcome, Topaz!"

"No, my inventions! They're gone! The last person I saw them with was this new girl, Coral. I need to find her and see if she's okay!"

"I hate to be the bearer of bad news, but sounds like to me that this 'new girl' stole your invention and entered it into the fair herself." Amber told her.

"Amber, must you always be so negative?" Ruby huffed.

"Well, let's go to the science fair and see. Either way Topaz isn't going to be able to enter the fair at this point anyways." Diamond said.

The rest agreed and they all made their way to the fair. They watched as different pegasus were setting up for the competition. Suddenly Topaz stopped and gasped. There, right in front of them, Coral was setting up her exhibit... with Topaz's inventions!
"I can't believe it, Amber was right! Coral stole my inventions!" Topaz frowned.
"I don't know why you're surprised. I'm usually right." Amber said.

Topaz stomped over to Coral. "Oh, hey Topaz! How do you like my new invention? It's paint that glows." Coral sneered.
"How could you do this to me?!" Topaz cried.
"Hmm, let's see. Maybe because this invention is amazing and all my ideas for the science fair wouldn't even compare! Now bye, bye! I need to finish setting up before the judges come!" Topaz frowned and angrily marched away.

"Aren't you going to do something?" Amber asked.

"There's nothing I can do but sit back and watch." Topaz told her. "I have no proof that the invention was mine. She stole everything." Topaz decided to stick around for the contest, even though her friends suggested they should leave. The judges soon made their way through the different exhibits, and eventually came to the final decision of the winner. As one of the judges stood up to make the announcement, Topaz held her breath.

"And the winner of this year's 'Best Invention Science Fair' goes to… Coral Reef!" The judge announced. People applauded while Coral bowed slightly and walked up to the judge.
"You win a scholarship to NAB University, along with credit to buy brand new science supplies!" He told her.
Topaz tried to hold back tears. That should have been her scholarship!
"I would like to thank all those that helped me make this invention possible!" Coral said while talking into the microphone. "I wouldn't have been here without your support."

163.

Topaz's friends offered to come sleep over but Topaz told them she wanted to be alone. That night, Topaz couldn't sleep. It just bothered her so much that Coral would do such an awful thing. Suddenly, she heard tapping at her window. Topaz got up and looked out. Under her window was standing Coral! Topaz frowned and flew down. "What are you doing here? Want to help me with another project?"

"No, Topaz, I need *your* help!" Coral said, distressed.

"HELP?! Why would I help you?!" Topaz asked angrily.

"Look, let me explain. I'm sorry for everything that happened, but I really need you. Lapus Lazuli, the famous fashion designer, was at the fair. He saw the invention and asked me to recreate it to use for his next fashion show… but I tried to recreate the paint and it's not working!"

"Of course not! Just in case, I left out one of the ingredients on the recipe. Good thing I did! Once someone like Lapus Lazuli finds out you can't make the paint, EVERYONE will know what a liar you are!" And with that, Topaz began to fly away.

"PLEASE FORGIVE ME TOPAZ!" Coral pleaded while grabbing her. "I know what I did was wrong, and I'm sorry! I promise never to do that again!"

"I don't want to hear it!" Topaz huffed.

Just then, the stone on Topaz's breastplate slowly started to fade.

"Wait! I was paid to do it!" Coral cried.

"Paid? By whom?" Topaz asked, turning around.

166.

"This guy named Chaos. He promised me all kind of awesome things and all I had to do in return was to steal your invention. But now I cannot live if I have to face the famous Lapus Lazuli and have him and probably the whole world find out what a liar I am! Please help me Topaz!"
"You made your choice! Go cry to Chaos!" And with that, Topaz flew back into her room and shut the window.

Finally, Topaz was able to sleep. It made her feel good to know that Coral was suffering because of what she did. Suddenly, a bright light shone through her window. Topaz squinted as she opened her eyes.

"Now what?" She yawned while looking out the window. There, standing below, was Prince Morning Star! "Prince Morning Star!" She gasped while hurrying down to him.

"Hello Topaz, I'm sorry for disturbing you in your sleep, but this could not wait." He smiled. "I'm here to talk to you about a pegasus named Coral."

"Oh, dreadful girl, I'm sure you heard what she did!" Topaz huffed.

"I did… and I heard what you did. That was not right to send her away. I want you to help her."

"What?!" Topaz exclaimed. "I'm sorry, you're Majesty, but what are you…"

"Your gift is mercy. Take a look at the stone I gave you. It lost its brilliance. That's because you are not using your gift. Mercy means to not give someone something they deserve. Maybe Coral deserves to be punished, but mercy forgives and forgets."

"She stole my invention Prince Morning Star! And she's working for Chaos!" Topaz cried.
"Not anymore. Coral has realized that Chaos just used her and then abandoned her, just like he eventually does to all who follow him. She needs to know mercy will help her through and that I am willing to accept her as my follower and take care of her always. Coral cannot see that unless you show it to her... for you are my little princess. I am counting on you." And with that, Morning Star flew away. Topaz sighed, knowing what she had to do.
"Is it always going to be this hard?" She asked aloud.

The next day, Coral got ready to have her meeting with Lapus Lazuli at the Gemstone Ballroom. She dreaded it, but knew she couldn't run. As Coral entered the ballroom, Lapus greeted her. "Ah, my dear Coral! So nice to meet you! I just went over some of the specifications with your assistant!" He told her.

"My assistant?" Coral asked, confused. Suddenly she turned and saw Topaz there.

"I hope you don't mind, but I already gave Lapus Lazuli the paint he ordered and began to talk about the details a little." Topaz smiled.

Coral was astounded. "Of course I don't mind, but…" Coral started, but then Lapus turned her toward a model.

"Look, look!" He said excitedly. The lights switched off and the model started to glow.

"Ah ha!" He jumped. "This will be the best fashion show ever! To Coral and her glowing paint!" The lights flipped back on.

"Hold on!" Coral stopped. Everyone looked at her. "This paint invention wasn't mine… it was hers!" She said while pointing to Topaz.

"She's not my assistant… I was hers!" Everyone was quiet.

"Well, that's true." Topaz said while walking next to Coral. "But the judges didn't know she was my assistant, so there was a mix-up. I stood in as the assistant today to not let this be an embarrassing situation."

"I'll make sure to give credit to whom it is due, but for now, I am just so excited about this paint! I will be ordering more from you in the future, yes?" Lapus said while turning back to his models.

"Wow, thanks Topaz. You're amazing!" Coral whispered.

"No… Morning Star is amazing. He was the one that told me to help you. He is such a wise and caring leader."

"Sounds like it! Not like that lying Chaos. I never want to listen to him again!" Coral said, and then something caught her eye. It was

Topaz's glowing stone! "Wow, what a pretty stone! Did you get it from the Prince?"

"It's a gift… inside is the power of mercy."

"You think I could get one too sometime?"

Topaz smiled. "Knowing Prince Morning Star, I'm pretty sure one day you will."

173.

Story Reflections
TOPAZ
Princess Of Mercy

It's so hard sometimes to forgive someone who did something bad to us! That's exactly what Topaz had a hard time with. It only makes sense that people who do bad things should be treated badly in return... but Jesus says the exact opposite. He said we should love our enemies and pray for those who persecute us! Jesus also said that it's not up to us to punish or judge those that wrong us... that's God's job. Our job is to forgive and love like God loves us and forgives us when we do bad things. Giving someone something good that they don't deserve is called mercy. If we show mercy to others, we will be a light to this world, because we can't have mercy unless God gives it to us first! So many people who were evil turned to God because they were shown mercy and love by his followers. If we do good to those that do bad to us, we are actually glorifying God and turning others to him.

Bible Verse:
"For if you forgive men their trespasses, your heavenly Father will also forgive you."
-Matthew 6:14

JADE
Princess Of Joy

The Pegasus Princesses had just landed from finishing a task for Prince Morning Star.
"Oh my, it is so tiring to fight against this Chaos sometimes." Ruby sighed. "It's so hard to stay humble!"
"Stop complaining!" Amber frowned. "It's not easy for any of us to use our gifts… except Jade. Joy comes naturally for her."
"Your right!" Jade jumped with joy. "I'm just lucky, I guess."
"Well, I better be getting home. I don't want my dad to worry. See you guys later!" Amethyst said while taking off.

"I think we all should get going. We'll keep in touch ladies!" Topaz said while flying off as well.
The others soon took off and Jade and Diamond were left together.

 "I guess I better get going too. See you tomorrow, Diamond!" Jade said, about to take off.

"Hey Jade, why don't I fly you home? My house is in that direction as well." Diamond told her.

"No!" Jade shouted anxiously.

Diamond stepped back, surprised by her response.

"I mean, it's okay. You don't want to fly me home."

"Why?"

"I just… I'm a little embarrassed about where I live… and my family."

"Oh, come on Jade. You're the Princess of Joy. It can't be that bad."

"I'd really appreciate it if you'd just let me go alone. Thanks." And with that, Jade zoomed off.

"That was weird." Diamond thought aloud. "Jade's living situation must be in a really poor condition. I have an idea!" She quickly raced after the other girls, hoping to catch them before they got home.

Jade looked back just to make sure no one was following her. She sighed with relief after seeing that that coast was clear. She slowly flew toward one of the richest cities in town, and landed in front of a large mansion. Looking up at the large house, she sighed and slowly punched in the gate code to let herself in.

As Jade entered the mansion, she looked around. Everything was quiet.
"Hello?" She asked, her voice echoing through the house. "Daddy? I'm home!"
No one answered. "He's probably at work. Figures."
Jade sadly walked up to her room. She looked around, not knowing what to do. Suddenly, an eagle flew into her room.
"Welcome home, miss." He said. "I'm sorry I did not answer right away. Can I get you anything?"

"Hi Charles. Is daddy at work?" She asked.

"I'm afraid so."

"Could you play a board game with me?"

"I'm afraid I don't 'do' games."

"Okay. Thanks anyways, Charles."

"You're welcome, miss."

And with that, he flew away.

"I hate being alone." Jade sighed. "It's so hard to have joy when no one is around. Everyone thinks it's easy for me... maybe sometimes, but not always."

"This had better be good, Diamond." Ruby frowned. "I would have been taking a relaxing bubble bath right now."

"Just hear me out... I think Jade is so poor that she is ashamed. I tried to fly her home and she says she is too embarrassed to have me see where she lives." Diamond told the girls.

"Oh, my. Poor thing." Amethyst sympathized.

"Maybe we can surprise her and bring her some gifts to cheer her up." Sapphire spoke up.

"Good idea!" Diamond agreed.

"Um, hello? We don't know where she lives! How can we surprise her? And won't it make her mad?" Amber spoke up.

"Oh, that part is easy. We can just call her and track her by her phone signal." Topaz told them.

"You can do that?" Amber asked.

"If I have to."

"It's settled then! Jade should realize that she shouldn't be embarrassed from her friends. It's our job to cheer her up!" Diamond announced. "We'll meet at Topaz's tomorrow early morning!"

"Who would have thought Jade would ever need to be cheered up?" Amber thought aloud as they all began to fly away. Little did they know that Chaos was spying on them, once again trying to figure out how to deceive them.

"Princess Jade… sad? What a lovely thought." He chuckled while slithering away.

Jade just hung up the phone with Topaz when she heard a knock on her door.

"Miss Jade?" It was Charles.

"What is it, Charles?" Jade asked, bored and sitting on her bed and playing with a ball.

"Someone is here to see you."

Jade perked up.

"Really? I'll be right down!" She said excitedly.

Jade raced down the stairs and saw a young pegasus standing in her living room.

"Who are you?" Jade asked.

"My name is Agate." He said. "I'm one of your new neighbors. I don't really know anyone here, and I was hoping we could be friends. I get kind of lonely sometimes."

"Me too! You could come here any time and we can hang out! I absolutely hate being alone, but daddy is always working and my mom… well, she left us."

"How about we play some games?"

"That would be awesome!"

Jade was so excited. Now that she had Agate close by, she would never be alone… and she would never be sad again!

Agate and Jade stayed up all night playing games and getting to know each other. Jade laughed when the sun began to rise.

"I can't believe we stayed up all night!" She chuckled.

"Yeah… and your dad still didn't come home." Agate added.

Suddenly Jade's heart sank.

"Yeah… you're right." She said sadly.

Her stone slowly started to fade from lack of joy.

"No wonder your mom left…" he kept going. "It must have been hard to have a husband like that who is never home."

186.

Jade's heart sank even more. Suddenly Charles flew in the room.

"Good morning, miss Jade…" He started. "There appears to be six young pegasus here to see you."

"WHAT?!" Jade exclaimed. "I told Diamond I didn't want anyone to see where I lived! How did they find out?"

"Your friends sound terrible." Agate spoke up. "They must have spied on you to see where you live. And what kind of friends would deliberately go against your wishes?"

"Not very good ones." Jade huffed angrily.

"Jade lives here?" Ruby exclaimed while looking up at the mansion. "If I would've known that I would have been friends with her a long time ago."

"Well, there goes our gifts. Nothing we brought would compare to what she has in there." Amber frowned.

"You guys, it doesn't matter. Jade needs to know that we're here for her. I'm sure she'll appreciate our effort." Diamond assured them. Suddenly the door opened and they saw Jade standing there.

"Jade!" Diamond exclaimed happily.

188.

"I told you not to come here!" Jade shouted.

"What?" Diamond was surprised by her reaction. "But I thought…"

"No, that's the problem, you weren't thinking. If you can't respect my boundaries, I cannot have you as a friend."

"Whoa… simmer down there, Jade." Amber spoke up.

"You be quiet, Amber! You always get to speak your mind, so let me speak mine! I thought you were my friends, but it looks like you're just too nosy about my life! Real friends wouldn't stick their noses where it doesn't belong."

"Jade, what is wrong with you?" Diamond asked softly.

"You are! How could you betray me like this, Diamond? I told you I was embarrassed about my life! I don't want to see any of you ever again!"

"But Prince Morning Star... he made us all his Princesses. We're like sisters. We can't break apart. We need to stay together."

"Where was Prince Morning Star all those times I've been alone? Where was Prince Morning Star when my mom left us? WHERE IS HE?! I QUIT!" Jade shouted while ripping off her breastplate and throwing it on the floor. "My life was better before I met you."

And with that she slammed the door.

The girls were all quiet.

"This was my idea... this was all my fault!" Sapphire whimpered.

"No, Sapphire, it's a good thing we came here." Diamond told them.

"Doesn't seem like it." Amber said. "We just lost one of the strongest members in our group. What is wrong with Jade?"

"I think I have a good guess." Topaz frowned. "Before Jade even started talking to us I noticed that her stone was black. We all went through times when we didn't use our gifts and our stones started to turn black... and we all know that Chaos or one of his minions were nearby all of those times, making sure we got discouraged."

"Chaos must be here." Diamond gasped. "We need to get to Jade as fast as possible!"

Jade angrily punched one of the couch pillows.

"Just let it out." Agate told her. "At least I'm here for you. What happened to the breastplate you were wearing?"

"I don't need it anymore."

"That is exactly what I wanted to hear." Agate chuckled. Suddenly, he morphed into a horrible dragon… the Dragon of Chaos!

"Chaos!" Jade gasped. "How dare you trick me! You'll be sorry!"

"Am I? I think you forgot that you just gave up any power to defeat me, and your friends are all gone. You have no one but me. But I come in peace. I don't like this whole good and evil battling type thing. Let's just have peace and be friends. Stick with me, and you'll never be alone. I got so many minions, I can make sure someone is with you at all times. And they can shapeshift and become any type of friend you want."

"What's going on in there?" Amber asked while Amethyst was peeking through the window.

"It's Chaos!" She gasped. "Jade is just talking to him."

"We need to get in there somehow!" Diamond said.

"We can't do anything unless Jade revives her stone." Topaz spoke up. "Without her, we can't defeat Chaos."

"Well, we'll make her put it on!" Amber said while picking it up, opening the window, and flying in the room.

"Here, Jade!" She called out while throwing her the breastplate. Jade looked down at it and back up.
"You still didn't leave?!" She said angrily.
"What is wrong with you? That's Chaos! We can't leave you alone with him!"
"Oh, but we are friends now. I will make sure Jade is never alone." Chaos smirked while putting his hand on Jade's shoulder.
"Chaos is my friend now. Now you leave before I have to make you!"
"No!" Amber shouted while the other girls flew in. Suddenly two shackles appeared around Jade's front legs.
"What's happening?" She asked.

194.

"One minor detail." Chaos chuckled. "You see, in order to be my friend and to take what I have to offer, you belong to me. No big deal. I'll make sure to keep you happy."

"Jade, what did you do?" Diamond asked sadly.

"But, wait, I changed my mind!" Jade said frantically.

"Too late, sweetheart. The deal is done. You are mine. You're coming with me." Chaos said while linking his shackles with hers. He started to fly away, pulling her with him.

"Help!" She called out.

"There's nothing they can do for you now." He told her.

Suddenly a voice boomed through the clouds. "CHAOS!" It called out. Everyone turned and saw Prince Morning Star flying toward them. "Let her go!"

"She made a deal with me! It's too late." He sneered. "It's over."

"It's over when I say it's over." Morning Star commanded. "Let my Princess go."

Then something happened. Chaos quietly unlatched Jade's shackles and flew away. Jade was stunned. She was in awe about how powerful Morning Star was… all he had to do was say the word and it sent Chaos away! As Morning Star approached her, she turned away. Jade couldn't bear to look him in the eye.

"It's alright, Jade." He told her softly. "I believe this is yours." He clasped her breastplate back on her. Jade was shocked.

"You mean… you are still taking me back? Even though I let Chaos trick me?" She asked.

"Chaos may say that I don't care, but that's a lie. I love you deeply. I love and care for all my subjects. That is why I need you and the other Pegasus Princesses to go out and let people know that I am always here, even though, like today, you didn't know it. I will never leave you alone. And because of that, you never have to be sad again."

Jade smiled as she came to Morning Star's side. Her stone began to flicker… until it lit up and shone brighter than it ever had before that day.

Story Reflections
JADE
Princess Of Joy

Even though joy is something that came naturally for Jade, there were times when it was still hard for her to be joyful. Just because we have a natural gift doesn't mean it's always easy to use. Like Jade, we also need to be careful when we are alone too much, because that's when Satan likes to play with our thoughts and trick us into thinking things that aren't true. It's good to share our thoughts with friends and family that care about us… and sometimes they might even help to point out bad thoughts we might have. One thing that is also very beautiful about following God is that, like Morning Star, Jesus is always there for us, watching over us. We might not always feel his presence, but for sure he is there and will never leave us alone as long as we follow him! Even if our life isn't exactly the way we want, we can be happy because we have a God who loves us and cares about us, and that's what really counts.

Bible Verse:

"Rejoice in the Lord always: and again I say, Rejoice."
-Philippians 4:4

www.anchristiancomics.com

Pegasus™ Princesses
PARABLES FOR KIDS

For Pegasus Princesses games, activities, videos, and a bunch of other cool free stuff, visit:

www.anchristiancomics.com

Under our "FREE STUFF" page!

About the Author

Arielle Namenyi was born in San Diego county, California, and currently lives there with her husband Norbert Namenyi and their children.

Having a passion for creating stories and characters, Arielle now creates books for the A.N Christian comics series that combines beautiful artwork with captivating stories and memorable characters.

"I was inspired to create the 'Pegasus Princesses' after searching for a Christmas present for my neice. I noticed there was not much Christian material for young girls that could compare to the non-Christian princess and pony material, so I thought it would be great to have a Christian alternative for young girls to enjoy."

Arielle's portfolio includes a number of illustrated and published works, animation, character design, logo and marketing designs, and much more.

For more books by Arielle Namenyi and her portofolio, visit:
www.anchristiancomics.com